Women Wide Awake

Stories, Sculptures, and Poems from Sindhi Folklore

Manahil & Nimra Bandukwala

MAWENZI
HOUSE

Published with the generous assistance of the Canada Council for the Arts and the Ontario Arts Council. We also acknowledge the support of the Government of Canada through the Canada Book Fund and the Government of Ontario through the Ontario Book Publishing Tax Credit.

Funded in part by Mississauga Arts Council's MicroGrant Program through the support of RAMA Gaming House - Charitable Gaming at City of Mississauga

Cover art and photography by Nimra and Manahil Bandukwala
Cover title embroidery by Huma Bandukwala
Artist photo by Ruqaiya Quettawala

Library and Archives Canada Cataloguing in Publication

Title: Women wide awake : stories, sculptures and poems from Sindhi folklore / Manahil & Nimra Bandukwala.

Names: Bandukwala, Manahil, author, artist, photographer. | Bandukwala, Nimra, author, artist, photographer.

Identifiers: Canadiana (print) 20230230598 | Canadiana (ebook) 20230230687 | ISBN 9781774151068 (softcover) | ISBN 9781774151075 (EPUB) | ISBN 9781774151082 (PDF)

Subjects: LCSH: Sindhi (South Asian people)—Folklore. | LCSH: Folklore—Pakistan—Sindh. | LCGFT: Folk literature. | LCGFT: Poetry. | LCGFT: Illustrated works.

Classification: LCC PS8603.A6185 W66 2023 | DDC C813/.6—dc23

Printed and bound in Canada by Coach House Printing.

Mawenzi House Publishers Ltd.
39 Woburn Avenue (B)
Toronto, Ontario M5M 1K5
Canada

www.mawenzihouse.com

To our family and chosen family, near and far

Contents

Mannat

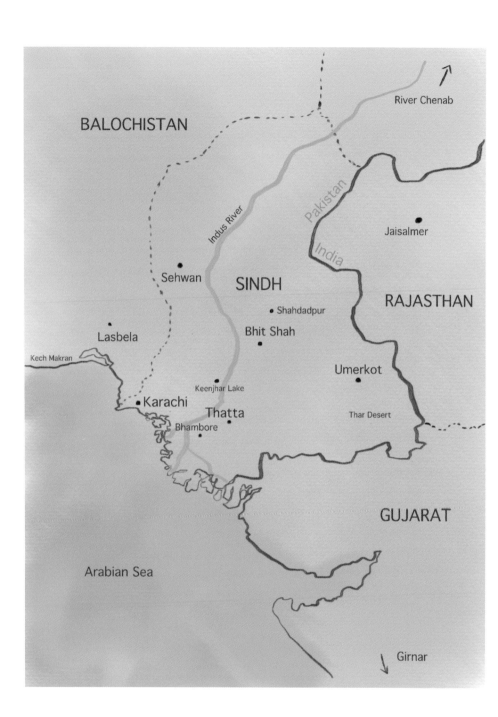

Preface

The stories, poems, and sculptures in this collection are based on stories from Sindh, Pakistan. They reflect our passions for crafting, poetry, and storytelling. Each story here is playfully retold and accompanied by a poem and a visual. To create the sculptures we have foraged from nature and from our family home in Karachi.

We were born and raised in Karachi but until this project knew very little about the stories from that region. In 2019 we travelled throughout Sindh to learn about these stories. In our travels, we learned that there is no one version of a folktale. Folklore travels geographically and evolves over time, and its forms depend on the culture, language, and context of any given place. This book is divided into three sections.

Passage is our interpretation of the stories of seven women from Sindh and surrounding areas. These stories emerged from a landscape steeped in a sense of spirituality and fate. Although they might end in what appears to be tragedy, the influence of Sufi, Islamic, and Hindu traditions means that death is not a definite end for the soul and the spirit. Through the music and stories of the eighteenth-century Sufi poet Shah Abdul Latif Bhittai, these women continue to be remembered. *Shelter* sails through the story of Karachi, from its humble origins as a fishing village to one of the largest cities in the world. *Mannat* ties together the relationships between the saints, people, and the folklore of the region by threading together the spirits of the stories and their tellers.

Each story includes a section called "Living Folklore," which gives *very* approximate notes about when and where it took place and where you can find the graves of the people that appear in it. Even today, people continue to visit the graves and shrines of the figures in these stories.

At the core of many of these narratives is the idea of union: with a beloved, with a community, and with the divine.

Folklore map of Sindh and surrounding areas

Passage

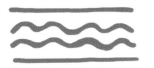

Unbaked
The Story of Sohni

Sohni's story drifted into Sindh through the River Chenab in Punjab. She lived by the river bank, from a family of kashigars, potters renowned for the sturdiness and intricacy of their earthenware. Sohni's practiced hands knew how to shape curves in clay with her eyes closed and paint intricate flowers in indigo, mustard, and white.

One day a trader named Izzat Baig came to the village to buy a pot. When the dark-haired stranger entered her shop, Sohni set down her brush and got up to help him. He selected a pot that had verses painted on it. With a smile, Sohni ran a blue-stained finger around the rim and told him she had composed them herself. Izzat Baig returned the next day to buy another pot, and similarly again the day after, and the day after that. Sohni struck up conversations with the handsome stranger, asking about life in the bustling cities. He asked her where she learned kashikari, and she shared stories of how her grandparents learned from their grandparents, and so forth. Days passed, and Sohni and Izzat Baig's flirtations grew from pining glances to long drawn-out exchanges. To be near Sohni, Izzat Baig started working as a buffalo herder in her village. He took the title of Mehar—buffalo herder—and their love blossomed.

But Sohni's parents did not approve of an outsider, and married her off to a local kashigar. They threatened Mehar and ordered him to leave the village. This slight complication did not deter him. He took his buffalos and settled down on the other side of the river. There, he was close enough to still lock eyes with Sohni as she sat hunched over her clay, streaks of white paint a shocking contrast with her dark hair. His buffalos grazed by the river bank while he basked under the sun for hours, the touch of Sohni's soft skin in his mind. He sang Sohni's verses as he worked, the raging river swallowing up his songs.

For her part, Sohni was not going to let minor setbacks like a husband or not knowing how to swim stop her from seeing the love of her life. Once the voices in the house settled into the quiet hum of snores, she

took a pot from the kitchen and snuck out. She used the pot to keep herself afloat as she paddled across the river. The thought of Mehar waiting for her on the other side pushed out any fears of water snakes wrapping themselves around her legs or the snapping sound that she told herself were sticks. Emerging from the dark water covered in muck, she approached Mehar. He took the shivering Sohni into his arms and held her tight, and had a pot of hot water and a lit fire waiting for her. The two stayed up until the first hint of light started to break through the sky. In the semidarkness, Sohni waded back across the river and tiptoed into her husband's bed before anyone woke up.

Their love grew with each passing night as they fantasized plans to escape. Sohni traced love poems on Mehar's back and he kissed her paint-stained fingers. Until one night, Sohni's sister-in-law saw her sneaking into the house before the sun was up. One woman pitted against the other, she stayed up the following night and saw Sohni stash her clay pot under the reeds that grew by the river. Her blood boiled and fogged her senses. Her father's and brother's voices echoed in her head and she stumbled into the shop, her hands grasping at clay. Sohni's baked clay pot was now replaced with an unbaked one.

Sohni waded into the river that night with her pot. She was halfway across when the clay caved under the weight of her arm. A wave washed over her head and she started to cough. Circling her arms around the pot, she grasped at the clay but it dissolved in the water. She lifted her head up and saw Mehar's figure waiting at the bank. He extended his arms out, inviting her embrace. Sohni flailed her arms and legs towards his fading silhouette. The smile on his face turned into a frown and his arms dropped to his side. He took a step forward and called out her name. She flung herself towards him, but her body gave out and she disappeared below the water. Mehar jumped to where Sohni was, but it was too late. Their bodies floated to the surface, the current carrying them to dimensions far beyond the village that kept them apart.

Living Folklore
Date: 18th century
Place: Along the River Chenab
Tomb: Shahdadpur, Sindh

Nocturne

Mehar calls these nights "Sohni raat"

like chand raat or Eid raat
where moon smiles from shadow
night where he watches the river for sighting
of me

we lie together
and pray at each other's altars. I make mine
from clay, he makes his from buffalo skull

*

fish nibble off the clay layer that collects
during my day in front of the potter's wheel,
think of me as algae
and rock

moon, she keeps my secret, stays
in shadow for three nights in the month. I sneak away

from house
                    from husband

riverbank squelches underfoot
a quicksand, lost in white water. elevate
my body with pot as life vest and kick
against the current

shallow rocks scrape my stomach
something curls around my foot

*

at the wheel today, my mother-in-law
wiggled a stick around
and called it a river snake

*

something slimy creeps up my leg
toes sink again and there is nothing
just algae and clouds of riverbank mud. water

black and white and every colour
but blue
heavy and dark and everything but gentle

krrtch, krrtch, krrtch

*

my sister-in-law said
there are crocodiles in this river
she dropped a pile of unbaked clay
its wet form settled around my feet

krrtch, krrtch. my father kicked a pile
of broken pot shards. krrtch. the sound

my husband makes
when I don't listen. krrtch

*

I am in a tunnel of rising water

rocks rise up and I land, loosen grip on my clay pot
wade with sari water-heavy
something wraps a scaly hand
around my ankle

washes off at the other end of the shore

Sohni in the River — Cloth, clay, found pot   9

*

It is Sohni raat. Mehar watches the river

but morning light breaks
he sees no
bobbing head. Just wet lumps
of clay stuck to rock

tangles could be hair or seaweed

he waits. at noon
blue water brings him

a clay pot
unbaked

The Necklace
The Story of Leela

Leela was the queen of Devalkot, an ancient city of Sindh. Witty, beautiful and married to King Chanesar, she had everything one could want. She loved accompanying him on his trips around Sindh. One of her favourite places included the ajrak workshops where men soaked block-printed cloth in madder and indigo dye. She could never resist getting dupattas from one shop, and a ralli quilt for her bed from another.

On one of their trips, Leela and Chanesar happened to visit a neighbouring kingdom, whose princess, Konru, set her eyes on Chanesar. The king, however, did not meet her eyes as she stroked his arm; he brushed it off and pressed his nose to Leela's forehead. But Konru was not one to give up so easily. Enlisting the support of her mother and the wazir of Devalkot, Konru embedded herself in Chanesar's court as Leela's servant.

One morning, she served Leela breakfast. She set the tray down and turned her head away. Leela caught a tear dripping down Konru's cheek and asked what was wrong. Half-acting, half-lamenting, Konru told Leela a fabricated version of her past. She had once been a princess but now was a lowly servant. All that was left as proof was a diamond necklace worth nine lakh rupees, so beautiful and bright it turned night into day.

This sounded impossible. Chanesar was the richest man around, believed to have accomplished all kinds of impossible feats, but Leela had never heard of jewelry that could conquer darkness. She demanded to see the necklace. With a sly smile, Konru fumbled with the square-shaped lump under her kameez and pulled out a box. Leela stood there tapping her foot, skeptical that this necklace could really outshine the night's full moon.

Konru opened the box, and all Leela saw was light. Her eyes adjusted, and there within hand's reach was the most magical thing she had ever seen. She had to have it. She begged Konru—she would give her more than nine lakh rupees. She would promote Konru to wazir—anything to

have the necklace. Konru was ready with her condition. Leela could have the necklace, if Konru could spend a night with Chanesar. A reasonable price. Leela said yes right away.

That night at dinner, Leela kept refilling Chanesar's wine cup. He drank and drank, until he stumbled to his room and collapsed on his bed. Konru walked in, blew out the sconces, and closed the door.

The following morning, Chanesar woke up and reached out to stroke his wife's hair. He recoiled at feeling the rough hair in his hand instead of the soft curls he expected. Turning over, with head pounding, he saw a smirking woman in his bed, reaching towards him. She was not Leela. The king pulled away but the woman said his lovely and devoted wife had traded him for a necklace.

Bile rose up in Chanesar's throat. The combination of wine and betrayal was too much. Wiping his mouth, he tore away his sheets and stormed through the palace until he found Leela curled up on a takht in the courtyard. His angry shout startled her awake. Leela lifted her head to see her husband looming over her, shouting at her to leave the palace at once. She darted her eyes to the side and saw the velvet box. Konru cocked her head and smiled as Leela shuffled her way to the palace gates, the necklace a collar around her neck. Konru seduced Chanesar into marriage, and Chanesar pushed away memories of Leela from his mind.

Leela went back to her family's village. On her way, the silver threads on her dupatta caught on thorns and rocks. Unable to stomach touching the necklace ever again, she dug at the hardened desert sand. Chanesar's fury whispered after her. Her nails bled but she kept digging, pleading words of forgiveness to the land. She threw the necklace into the deep hole. Rising up from the ground, she kicked sand on top of the diamonds. Her neck felt lighter, but the weight of her choices remained. There was still a long way to go, but a gentle breeze brushed against her sweaty forehead.

Living Folklore
Date: 14th century
Place: Devalkot, Sindh (near to what is now Thatta)
Tomb: Unknown

Cloves and Cotton

Konru was a planner. she didn't think
just a necklace would seduce Leela away

      the necklace just a ruse

other palace maids walked around the strange
new girl who chanted over cloves and salt
and strung up in the pantry
cotton threads laced with orange peels

if these spells actually worked
none of them would be here pressing
the king's sheets but they let her dream

the girl who ripped the king's silk pants
during laundry, kitchen knife left a clean cut
      silk flowed out of her unpracticed hands
someone teach the new girl how to sew

fingers pricked bloody, smeared on a rock pile
she kept in the corner of her room. Konru

marked the days off on a wet cement slab
      in one week Chanesar will be mine
written with water. she slipped petals
between the king's fork and watched him eat

just a necklace seduced Leela away
      a necklace of dull rocks and crumbling bush

      Leela left the palace with rocks and chewed up flowers

A Lovers' Mausoleum
The Story of Sasui

Her story begins with the stars. Sasui was born near Sehwan, in northern Sindh, a daughter of Hindu Brahmins. At Sasui's birth, astrologers predicted that she would marry a Muslim. By this time, a considerable number of Muslims had settled in Hindu-majority Sindh. To abandon the highest social class was unacceptable, and Sasui's parents knew they had to get rid of the child or risk becoming ostracized by their Brahmin caste. The easiest way to get rid of a child was to put it in a basket and let the basket float down the river.

The baby made her meandering journey past the sand dunes, the sun burning down through the gaps in the woven basket. Water splashed through the reeds and soaked into the coarse cloth wrapped around her. She cried the entire way down. A passing hunter cocked his gun, thought the cry came from a jackal but didn't see the basket. Eventually, soiled and sunburned, Sasui washed up on the banks of Bhambhore.

Bhambhore was a dhobi ghat, a village of washerpeople. The chief took the baby in and named her Sasui.

*

Sasui was an adult now. Traders from Kech Makran, in the province of Balochistan, often travelled up to Bhambhore. One of these men was Punhoon, son of the Muslim king of Kech Makran. The stars said it, and so it happened.

Sasui and Punhoon got married, but Punhoon's father was against his son marrying a village girl, even if she was the chief's daughter. The king sent Punhoon's brothers to bring him back. They came to Bhambhore with wine and pretended to celebrate. Punhoon drank so much wine that he passed out. His brothers hoisted him onto a camel and snuck him out of Bhambhore in the middle of the night. Sasui woke up to find her husband gone.

This deception could not go against the stars. Sasui set out to find her husband. Barefoot, she walked hundreds of kilometres in scorching days and frigid nights through the deserts of Sindh all the way to the rugged mountains of Balochistan. She let her instinct lead the way. There was no rain or food; thorns pricked the soles of her feet and left red trails of blood on the sand. The sun burned her face and cracked her smooth skin until she looked old.

*

Her days of wandering found her at Lasbela in Balochistan. Exhaustion finally overtook her and she fell to the ground. Sasui prayed for a miracle. The stars answered as she ran over the mountains. A hill split into two and she slipped inside. The ground closed above her. Her dupatta caught in a crack, waving red against the muted desert.

*

In Kech Makran, Punhoon's restless melancholy convinced his father to let him go back to Sasui. Punhoon rode through Lasbela and on the way saw a fresh grave. The red cloth flapping in the wind was surely a marker of a saint's passing. Kneeling down, he prayed to be united with Sasui again. The hill split open once again, swallowing Punhoon.

And so the stars won.

Living Folklore
Date: Unknown
Place: Bhambhore, Sindh
Tomb: Near Lasbela, Balochistan

Through Saltwater and Thicket

from Sehwan to Bhambhore

if you asked me what it was like

to swim down a river
from one end of a province
to the other

I could not tell you

there was sweetwater
and Sindhu dolphins nudged
my basket along

criss-crossed wood kept my baby-face
from the sun. Fast-moving
current pushed me southwards

so all I could do
was keep moving on
no clouds a benchmark of time

saltwater jumps in and stings
my eyes

I could cry and cry but the thing
about the rivers is they are loud

catch a chill and who
would miss me

no hug from someone who loves me

from Bhambhore to Lasbela

if you asked me what it was like

to walk across a desert
cross boundary
of a province

I could not tell you

not when each footstep slowed
and slowed till I could not
feel movement

my face has aged twenty years
and I cannot recognize
my feet under oozes of black pus

so all I could do
was keep moving on
no clouds a benchmark of time

blood covered with sand that blew
into my eyes

rags I wear at noon do nothing
to protect me at midnight

catch a chill and who
would miss me

no hug from someone who loves me

just course fibres made
in haste. I could claw

my way out but someone
sent me down a river
before my bones
fully formed

I was not meant to survive
in this small space but its walls
have kept me safe
despite it all

just two cold walls
on either side. I could dig

a hole here and scrub
this skin clean, iron against
baked patch where the sun
beats down

I was not meant to survive
in this small space but its walls
have kept me safe
despite it all

The Lyre of Fate

The Story of Sorath and Rai Dyach

To welcome the new addition to their family, King Rai Dyach brought a face reader to look at his sister and her newborn son. Reading the baby's bright eyes and puckered mouth, the face reader could have predicted riches and joy that the young one would bring to the kingdom. Instead, the reader looked at the slope of the boy's nose, and gave an ominous warning: the boy would grow up to kill his uncle.

Rai Dyach's sister would not risk her brother's life for a baby that did not even have a name yet, so she wrapped him up and placed him in a basket and sent him down the river. The baby ended up in the neighbouring kingdom, where he grew up on the outskirts of the forest playing music for all the animals around.

Two decades later, the prophecy was far from Rai Dyach's mind. He had just married Sorath, a woman from a neighbouring kingdom. He lay in bed with his new wife, stroking her dark hair and intertwining his fingers with hers. A sweet tune floated through the open window. Sorath kissed her husband's knuckles, her heart feeling light at the charmed look on his face.

Rai Dyach pushed himself off the bed and leaned over the window ledge. Below, a young man sat on a rock, strumming a lyre. The palace cats sat in front of him, a captivated audience. The king jumped up in a flash of inspiration. He called out to Sorath to get dressed and come to the courtyard immediately and bolted out of the room. Her husband had his quirks, Sorath mused, as she pulled her shalwar on.

In the courtyard, Sorath leaned against her husband's shoulder as the man with the lyre entered. He introduced himself as Bijal from the neighbouring kingdom. The king invited him to stay in the palace and play music there forever. The king would give the musician anything. Gold, power, the finest assortment of instruments.

Bijal said, his mouth puckered, that he wanted one thing: Rai Dyach's head.

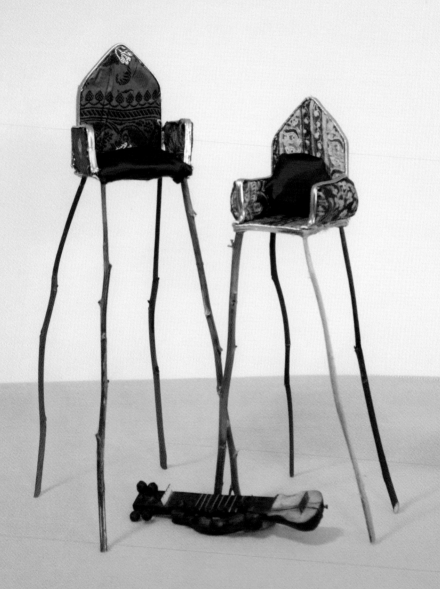

The courtyard fell silent, until Sorath's gasp broke the moment. She looked over at her husband, ready for him to order this man be thrown out of the kingdom. But Rai Dyach's head slowly started to tilt downwards. Sorath tugged his hand and pulled her husband upright. She stared at him, willing him to refuse.

But Rai Dyach shook his head. He pulled his hand out of Sorath's grip and stood up. Unsheathing his sword, he bowed his head to the musician. With a tug of his hand at his own throat, the sword sliced through and his head tumbled down, landing at Bijal's feet. Fate had played her hand.

Living Folklore
Date: Unknown
Place: Girnar, Junagardh District, Gujarat
Tomb: Unknown

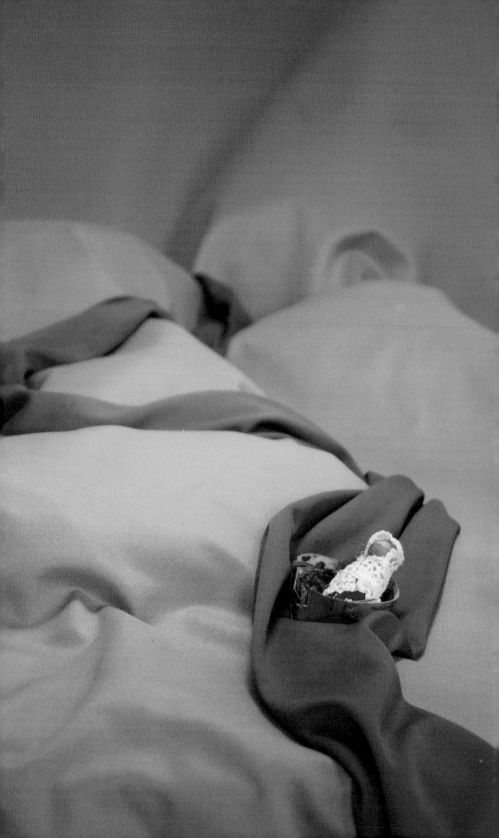

If Someone Had Said

no one said it was easy
to let your own child go
down the river. no one
said she chose her brother
over her son. no one said
this wouldn't work at all.
no one said she should
have thrown the baby
into a fire and watched
its bones become ash. no
one said the baby would
not have burned at all.
no one said it was fate
strumming its own lyre.
no one said fate could be
a liar. no one said fate
would be stronger than
his queen's pleas. no one
said war was without
blood. no one said the
aftermath would not be
a funeral pyre setting
the palace aflame, queen,
musician, lyre and all

Baby in Basket – Cloth, birch bark, rose petals, lace

A Chadar from Maleer

The Story of Marvi

Marvi's love story is part of the soil that shaped her. She lived in Maleer, a village in the Tharparkar desert. She spent her childhood sliding around on sand dunes and playing hide-and-seek behind the squat date trees. As she grew older, the desert winds defined her sharp features and the sun's light glowed off her face. A man from her village fell in love with her. She adored him, her family, and the people of her village. Listening to stories at night, watching the constellations shine, there was nowhere else she would rather have been.

But the petty jealousy of a boy was about to devastate her life. He worked for her father, and made advances towards Marvi, but she was not interested. The scorned boy, hungry for revenge, went to Umer Soomro, the king of Umerkot, and waxed poetic about Marvi's beauty. He suggested that Umer make Marvi his queen.

And that is exactly what Umer did. The very next morning Umer rode to Maleer on his strongest camel. Marvi was crouched over the village well drawing water, her chadar wrapped around her shoulders, when Umer came along. He grabbed Marvi by the waist and hoisted her up onto his camel. During the entire ride back to Umerkot, he imagined proposing to Marvi, and could picture her beautiful face as she lay on his adorned bed.

But Marvi struggled against his grip all the way to the fort; she squeezed her eyes shut when he pointed out her village; she turned her face away when he lay jewels down at her feet. Umer vowed he would find a way to make Marvi his wife. But Marvi refused him. He had money, power, jewels—everything. He kept Marvi in a small room in Umerkot Fort, visiting every day with a new jewel. Still she refused him.

Marvi turned her back on all the chests of gold jewels Umer brought for her. She did not wash her hair with rose or jasmine water as the people of the palace did. Greasy locks hung around her greying skin. Her coarse chadar frayed at the edges. She threatened to set the room on fire and burn herself inside.

Years passed. Marvi's chadar was more hole than cloth, but she still hugged this one memory of Maleer around her wasted body. She longed for the hot sand of her home. Only this hope kept her alive, year after year.

One day, without warning, an impatient knock on the door startled her. Umer's servant entered and, without explanation, informed her that there was a horse outside, waiting to take her back to Maleer. The servant left the small door of Marvi's prison open. She tentatively took a step out, expecting Umer to jump out from around the wall and throw another diamond at her feet, but no one came.

She mounted the horse at the fort entrance and was ready to ride off, when the tall, imposing figure of Umer approached. He held up his hands in surrender, and Marvi knew this was no trick. She could finally go home.

But Marvi's village did not welcome her back with the same fervour she kept for it. Having spent so long in Umerkot, Marvi's fiancé and her parents did not believe that she had not been tainted. Umer got her into this mess, so Umer had to get her out of it.

Umer offered to face a trial to prove Marvi's chastity. He and Marvi both held their hands to a hot iron rod. When they released the rod, their hands were unscathed. This was enough proof of their innocence, so the village took Marvi back.

Living Folklore
Date: 12th century
Place: Umerkot and Maleer (historical village near Umerkot), Thar Desert, Sindh
Tomb: Unknown

Necessary Tests

1.
an elder heats a rod over a fire stoked by shrubs

the village gathers
to watch the rod turn from grey to red

the elder beckons and I
step forward. I clasp rod with palm burned
over cooking fire. release. it falls

and hisses on the soil. skin
heals. Umer

steps forward too. the elder does not discriminate

Umer clasps the hot rod with hands
scraped from clutching
his horse's reins. he too comes away
unscathed

2.
do you know how to swim?
the elder asks

shake my head. *good.* he beckons
me to jump into the river

but I just said I don't know how to swim.
the elder pushes me along

your chastity will help you float. I frown
at the river's edge, hand
skimming cold surface

I don't think that's how it works. I jump

and look at that —

the elder is right. kameez
balloons out in the water. wet face
catches evening chill. a village boy

pulls me out. I shiver; someone
(not my husband) brings a blanket

I pick up the hot iron rod to warm my hands

3.
I enter a room
filled with shrubs and a wheel. the elder
leaves me here

where I cannot emerge until
I have turned the shrubs to gold. only someone
chaste could accomplish such a feat. I mutter

*Maleer would be a very different village
if we could do that* but take a seat
in front of a pile of shrubs and set wheel
into motion. noon sun is at its peak

shrubs shine in gold strands. I
show the elder with village as witness

he locks the shrubs away in a room
where they dull back to brown again

4.
I could keep going
with these miracles
that ultimately
prove nothing

A Feast of Fish Bones

The Story of Noori

Noori was from a fishing village near Keenjhar Lake, in Thatta. She grew up in a vibrant, close-knit community, knotting ropes into nets and gutting fish. At the end of the night, when the last fish bone was picked clean and the nets were hung out to dry, she would sit at the edge of the lake illuminated blue in the moonlight.

One day, Jam Tamachi, the ruler of Thatta, went hunting in the woods on the edge of the lake and ended up in Noori's village to rest for the night. Curious, Noori perched herself near the hut where the king was staying. Was his hair truly made out of gold, as the stories went? Did he have layers of necklaces strung around his neck, heavy enough that he always walked with a hunched back?

She craned her neck as Jam Tamachi left the hut. Just then, the Jam turned and locked eyes with her. Noori admired his tall stature and he was spellbound by her dark locks. Noori approached the Jam. The first thing she uttered was, "Have you ever tasted seared catla fish?" Jam Tamachi smiled and shook his head. "Come," he said, and they spent the night at Keenjhar Lake, talking and laughing as they splashed their feet in the cool water. By the time dawn broke, Jam Tamachi asked Noori to marry him.

She went to Thatta with him and lived in his palace as his seventh wife. Noori was surrounded by wealth. But her simple cotton kameezes stuck out amidst the delicate silks of the palace, and her neck and ears remained bare of jewelry. Jam Tamachi often found her curled up on the hard floor of the palace courtyard. Sometimes he would wake her up, and the two would talk under the stars.

This aroused jealousy in Jam Tamachi's other wives, and they conspired to discredit Noori in Jam Tamachi's eyes. Once they told the Jam that Noori was stealing money from the palace. Every night, Noori went to the palace gardens and gave her brother a wooden box. The wives told the Jam that the box was full of jewels. Noori, who refused to wear a gold crown? Was it all an act? Confused and betrayed, the Jam decided to find out the truth.

He caught Noori's brother entering the palace one night, and demanded he show the king the box. Jam Tamachi opened the box to find it full of fish bones and bread scraps. Bewildered but relieved, he asked Noori about it the next day. In her soft voice, Noori explained that she did not want to get used to the taste of tender meat and fresh prawns for fear that she would stop loving the food from her mother's hands. Thus the wives' schemes would end in the Jam's love for Noori growing even more.

When Noori died, Jam Tamachi buried his beloved wife in the middle of Keenjhar Lake. Her small white tomb sits there today, peeking out during low tide. People from her village boat out to the tomb and sprinkle flowers on her grave rising from the blue water that Noori always took pride in.

Living Folklore
Date: 14th century
Place: Thatta, Sindh
Tomb: Keenjhar Lake, Sindh

A Village Remembers

every August for seven hundred years
monsoon rains have come. and when they come

they wash up fish bones and bread scraps
in Keenjhar Lake. sweetwater knows the woman
who lies in its middle, feeds her

a feast like a brother brings a sister. every August
the lake rises. some shrines

sit atop hills to test the strength of pilgrims' legs
others are in deserts to see
how long they'll go
without water. this one lies

in the middle of a lake to see how much
a village can swim. fish

find themselves swallowed and spit out
by crocodiles. a city
chokes itself into amnesia

but a village remembers to set out
coarse bread and a day to sail out to a tomb
in the middle of a lake and tell stories

of the time Noori went on a date with a king
without so much as a necklace

or when she moved her pillow
outside so she could sleep on sand, looking up
at the waning crescent moon

Noori and Ships – Dupatta, wedding invitations, clay, cardboard   39

The Sisters' Labyrinth
The Story of Moomal

Popularly known as the love story of Moomal and Rano, we like to think of it as the story of the sisters Moomal and Soomal. The two sisters had used their wits to lure rich men. Running in fear of their lives then, Soomal built the Kaak Mahal, the palace of illusions in the Rajasthan desert. It was a place with glass lakes and lush green conifers, surrounded by sand and scorching heat.

Soomal started a rumour across the desert about a princess whose beauty was comparable to the stars. Princes and soldiers came to the palace to glimpse the elusive Moomal, but none made it through the trials and tests of Kaak Mahal.

Men would enter the palace and meet Natar, a servant who would lead them into the heart of the garden. There they were left alone. At first all looked fine. They left trails of gold coins from their pockets to make sure they did not lose their paths. But night soon fell, and so commenced the slithering and hissing and growling. Moving shadows darkened their path. Natar watched from her vantage point above the labyrinth's hedges as the men pulled out their swords and hacked at the air. They ran through the twisted trails, thorny kankera trees on the paths.

Thirsty men stumbled to a lake. Crouching down, they stuck their tongues out, ready for the cool water to soothe their parched throats, only to touch glass instead. Once their cries for help dwindled and their bodies stilled, Natar scooped up the gold coins and brought them to Moomal and Soomal.

A man who made his way out of the labyrinth strode into the palace one day ready to claim his prize. Exhausted, his gaze fell upon some beds on which he could rest his aching limbs while he waited for his princess. Without a care, he threw down his sword and collapsed on one of the beds. Instead of the relief of a soft mattress, he fell right through the sheet, under which was a deep well.

Natar added the fine swords of the fallen men to the ever-growing pile

of wealth in the middle of the palace.

A handful of fortunate men slept on the one bed out of the seven that was woven out of fiber instead of loose string. He woke up refreshed, but saw no princess at his feet. Sword in hand, he crept up the narrow stairs. Something appeared in front of him. He brandished his weapon at the figure, but all he heard was a clank. Dropping his sword, he darted his eyes around, only to be met with twelve faces peering back. He stepped back to escape but was met with his own frightened face. The only way out was ahead, but ahead was a row of a hundred more reflections. He turned a corner, then another. Another hundred appeared. Eyes closed, he extended his arms in front. Cool glass was his only compass as he treaded forward. His stubbled face grew into a full beard—the only marker of time passing.

Of all the men who ended up in deep wells and endless mirror mazes, only one defeated his own mind and journeyed into the heart of the palace. He was Rano, a minister from Umerkot. He glimpsed Natar's pink dupatta at the top of the maze in the garden. At every corner, the mirror's edge had a flash of pink. The pink was his sign through the endless trials, the last test through fire that was cool to touch. Whether it was his adrenaline from seeing a person after weeks alone, or her surprise at seeing someone break through Soomal's illusions, Moomal fell in love with Rano, and he with her.

Their wedding was a beautiful, private affair, witnessed by Soomal and Natar. Afterwards Rano went to Umerkot alone, prepared to comfort his worried wife. He told her that he was lost riding through the Thar desert, but made no mention of the magnificent palace and the remarkable princess that he married. He waited until his wife was asleep and then rode back to the Kaak Mahal to Moomal. By morning, his speedy camel had him back in Umerkot, in bed with his wife.

Rano arrived at Kaak Mahal at the same time each night. He and Moomal spent night after night in each other's arms, talking about everything . . . well, not everything. Rano kept his mouth shut about his wife, evaded Moomal's questions about his parents, and brushed off her inquiries about when she would see his home in Umerkot.

A night came when Rano still had not arrived. Without him in her bed, Moomal was unable to sleep. She nudged her sister awake and asked

her to sleep beside her.

The sky was almost light outside when Rano finally arrived. He saw another figure in Moomal's bed. Hurt and betrayed, he threw his walking stick on the floor and stormed off. He rode back to Umerkot, reliving the trials of thorns, shadows, and self.

When she woke up, Moomal saw Rano's stick, and knew what he had seen and thought. If only Rano had woken her up, or she had stayed awake! If only he had taken her to his home in Umerkot. If only he—but it was too late. Her lover was gone, and Moomal knew in her heart that he did not intend to come back.

Living Folklore
Date: 16th century
Place: Lodhrava, Rajasthan (now Jaisalmer)
Tomb: Unknown

Dream Doors

the woman gives me a drink, sweet candied thick with scent. sand dusted
along my neck   my camel led away, swords stripped off
left just me   a lush forest I step into it. desert sun burns through
flimsy canopy.   desert moon brings out the shadows
the hisses   the roars   shape ready to pounce   .
my kurta catches in thorns   bottom rips off   I run and trip into
glass   lay back and beg   the
sky   relieve me   (it does no such thing)   so I hoist
myself up and spin in circles   till I see it
pink   .   eyes open just enough to follow her
past the animals   desert sand follows me inside a hall   I
need   I need to lay down and rest for a minute
I wish it   it appears   lay down and close my eyes
      (brief relief).   wake to see on
another bed another prince   he collapses down and down and the
room is empty   peer down into a well   his
body so many bodies   mine has been spared (keep moving).
a flower to present a princess except when I touch it I shrink and these
are not ants but shrunken men and sand too slippery for me to run
must be days I spent   . out of this maze for my feet now one for my eyes
everywhere I turn is me   me with hair tangled muddy brown   me
with shirt more shred than cloth   what princess would look and say
yes   a staircase that climbs and climbs   (is
the princess even real)   (is the princess even kind)
                              I could turn back or die with this man
who lies on the steps   .   a flash of pink. I
muster on

Follow Her – Reclaimed dupatta, Rooh Afza sharbat, jute, pistachio shells, rocks   47

Seven

a tree grew feathers and flew
to the heavens
left a lake-shaped hole —

no, this is not the right folklore

a woman did not know how to swim
but knew how to float across the River Chenab
and this was enough

a woman walked across a desert
from Bhambhore to Lasbela,
no shoes, no water, to find her love

a woman loved her soil
more than anything
a king could give her

a woman had to run so she hid
in a house of puzzles that men who wielded swords
could not break through

a woman traded her husband
for a necklace
and regretted it

a woman became a queen
but ate fish bones and bread
despite the chests of jewels around her

a woman's skeleton lies covered
by centuries of blown

Seven Queens – Dried flowers, watercolour, paper

desert wind and sand

by magical lake I mean

the moon as the moon pushes
and pulls the tide and a woman's tear

as a tear
evaporates
into nothing

Shelter

The Bartenderess

The Story of Mokhi

Remember Natar, the maidservant at Kaak Mahal, from the story of Moomal? Well, after Moomal left the palace and there was no need to maintain the illusions, Natar had to find somewhere to go.

During the fourteenth century, saaki khanas were a popular place for people to get together after a long day of work. They would spend the evening lounging on takhts and pillows while drinking wine fermented from dates and grains. Natar, with her entrepreneurial spirit, opened up a saaki khana in what is Karachi today. Her famous wine was aged in matkas, the cool clay keeping it chilled for the thirsty patrons who stumbled into the brewery every evening. Her daughters worked there too.

One of Natar's daughters, Mokhi, often served a regular group of men—Mataras, or strong, hefty men. The Mataras loved the wine that Natar made and often came to the saaki khana.

On one of their visits, Mokhi told them that it happened to be off-season and she did not have anything to serve them. The Mataras brushed off Mokhi's words, saying that she must have something tucked away in a corner. Mokhi went to the celler to see if there was an overlooked pot there. In a dusty corner she found a jug of wine. The men were blown away by the taste and asked Mokhi where she had hidden this divine juice. It was better than anything they had had before. By the time they left, there was not even a drop left for Mokhi to taste.

After they had left, Mokhi started cleaning up. She picked up the jug, and almost dropped it. At the bottom of the clay vessel she saw a coil of bones. Snakes slithered around the saaki khana all the time—one must have fallen into the jug and fermented into the exquisite taste that the Mataras had obsessed over. Mokhi worried about the men. Would something happen to them from that wine? She waited for news to come, but none arrived.

The new season came, and so did the Mataras. When Mokhi saw them sauntering in, she breathed a sigh of relief. She walked up to the men with

a smile and offered the newest selections. But the men refused and asked for the wine she had served them the last time. Mokhi, fed up, yelled out the secret of the wine. As soon as they heard this, their faces grew pale and they collapsed.

The Mataras' graves are still in Karachi, in Gadap Town, the graves of the strong men. Mokhi did not kill them—it was their own fear. Their strength could not save them from their imaginations.

Living Folklore
Date: 16th century
Place: Gadap Town, Karachi, Sindh
Tomb: Gadap Town, Karachi, Sindh

Fear's Curse

the first thing I knew was green sand and the last was red wine

hatched in a palace that dissolved
in my adolescence I was left

to find a new home. The palace architect
followed her sister so I clung to the other wanderer
we traversed a desert

from one northern point to the southern
edge, where I learned the true colour

of sand as it settled into my scales
and the strength of fermented grapes. untouchable

the two of us, with my bared
fangs and Natar's powerful juice. I had a sip once
and was left a dangling scarf
around her neck until I woke once again

but a sip I craved again and again. We ceased being travellers
at the edge of an empty road. I could have pulled
her along but Natar said

no, this is where I will raise my daughter. and we did,
once, twice, a third time

around. I flicked my tail through the house until

the house became inhabited
by men
who would have sliced through me
before I could slither away. I was left

Snake and the Mataras' Graves — Bones, shells from Karachi's coast,   57
rose petals, laminate

to find a new home in dark corners in the cellar. Here
I indulged more than a few sips, a few

                      more

                         a few

A Woman Wide Awake
The Story of Mai Kolachi

What is Karachi? Unlike historic cities of folktales like Thatta and Umerkot, Karachi's story is pieced together from rushed responses to the question, *What is Karachi?* The largest city in Pakistan should have a grand story of how it came to be. Heroes, forts, drama, and adventure— not so much. Before the eighteenth century, Karachi was a small fishing village on the coast of the Arabian Sea. Here, women took charge of the day-to-day domestic matters while the men went out to sea to catch food.

In those days going away for an extended trip was nerve-wracking for those left behind. The women had no contact with the men for weeks, no way of knowing if the waves had taken their men under or creatures from the water had emerged to attack the boats. The only way for the anxiety and fear to lift from their hearts was for the boats to appear on the horizon.

One day when there had been no sign of the men for a long time, one woman stepped up and said she would go out to sea to find them. This woman was Mai Kolachi. She sailed upon the waters, determined to find her husband. In other stories, she had sailed to find her son, Moriro, and save him from a crocodile. The story often ends with her taking the role of the village head.

Unlike other folktales from Sindh, which have historical records, marked gravestones, and still extant sites, Mai Kolachi left little evidence behind. But what her story tells us is that when Karachi wanted to construct its identity, it chose to do so through the character of a woman, who gave the place its name.

Karachi has grown rapidly in the past 200 years, from a small fishing village to a city of almost fifteen million. It drew in over a million migrants after the Partition of the Subcontinent and has significant numbers of almost every ethnic group in Pakistan. In the face of the unknown, Mai Kolachi let go of her restlessness and unease and let her resilience carry her forward. Karachiites have taken up this mantle of resilience

against political instability and environmental catastrophes whether there is truth in the story of Mai Kolachi or not.

Living Folklore
Date: 17th century
Place: Kolachi Port, Karachi, Sindh
Tomb: Unknown

The Illusory City

before there is anything there is sea, salt, and sand

before Hindus carve deities into crowning
and Parsis sit at desks and draw blueprints
new Memon masjid sits where two roads meet
Gujratis trade everything from paper to perfume

there are fishermen sprinkled along the coast
they tell their children about a woman

what did she look like?

tall, must have been tall

if a highway bears her name. dark wisps of hair
always peeked out under her dupatta

so she wore shalwar kameez like we do

yes, absolutely
and all the way to her elbows were thick bangles

because she was Mai, respected lady

what did she like to do?

sit in the sand and watch
the horizon turn orange, make sandcastles
and sandmonsters, pet turtles that crawl

up the beach and release hatchlings
back into the sea. adventure, too, though this

necessity, instead of the rush of riding a boat out beyond
the shore's line of sight

she must have been brave

to go without knowing anything

all the migrants who reached Karachi
and all the ones who followed after

anything could happen out there, but it did not matter

she got there, and back
after all

Current

The Story of Moriro

Truer than the story of Mai Kolachi but less remembered is the story of Moriro and the magarmach. We are still in a fishing village called Kolachi in the eighteenth century, but this time the threat is from outside forces. Off the coast at Clifton was a whirlpool called Kalachi jo Kun. A magarmach-like monstrous creature made its home in the vortex, making daily meals of villagers on passing boats. The few who escaped described the creature's snapping teeth, glaring yellow eyes, and colossal size. One villager said its scales were green, another swore the monster was the dark red of blood.

Moriro was the youngest of seven brothers. All of them were muscular and tall except Moriro, who was physically disabled, always teased, and treated like a child. His brothers would leave him behind when they went out to sea, sure that he would not be able to defend himself against the magarmach. A time came when his brothers did not return. Splinters of wood from their boat washed up on the shore. Moriro's brothers had faced the crocodile and met their end.

Moriro resolved to avenge his siblings. He designed an elaborate cage covered with spikes that only emerged when someone pulled a lever. The village ironsmiths built the cage. To pull the cage out of the water, sixty bulls were tied to it with ropes while he sat inside as bait. The magarmach smelled the fresh bait in the water and swam towards it. It opened its jaws to swallow the cage, when Moriro pulled the lever. Spikes shot out and forced the monster's mouth open. The bulls pulled Moriro and the dead magarmach out of the water. The villagers cut the creature open and found the remains of Moriro's brothers, who were all buried at Gulbai Chowk, where their graves still remain today.

Living Folklore
Date: 18th century
Place: Kolachi, Karachi, Sindh
Tomb: Gulbai Chowk

Moriro in Cage and the Magarmach – Twigs, bark, shell, bone, clay, cloth   67

Dis-sheltered

most good stories begin underwater. at the end of this
I will have one to tell. it cycles between calm and uncalm

heartbeat I pace to match. the whale is a crocodile
it snaps up bones as it swallows. the crocodile is a dog

it smells fear. I must be fearful. it must come to meet
me here. on a rock that juts out of the seafloor I incise

my forearm. like a shark the crocodile comes at scent
of blood. water ripples. it's coming. I inhale again

just me this time. it came quickly and took away a brother
before I had time to exhale. it doesn't know how to swim

just to float until the whirlpool spins it in and ships fly
into its mouth. in the worst moments of me and my mind

alone and waiting I picture my ribs floating into
my brother's. absent of flesh we form our own cage, unwhole

but still together. seven brothers in a line morph
into a crocodile. it's here, for real this time. down its throat

I see flashes of white bone. I clutch what could be
a brother's hand. he pulls me to the lever

I was not made to die here
with saltwater and coral growing out of my skull

Mannat

Vigil

The Marhun Machi, a creature of the water

I wait for my lover.

The first time I held her against my chest, seasons and seasons ago, she took my cold hands and said, *my cheek heats from the warmth of your heart.* I said, *I'll carve open a passage for you to keep the cold seafloor at bay. No need*, she said, and pulled out a vial of sunlight. *I found this on the coast. This is what shone through the clear water the day I first saw you. This is what kissed your face.* She stroked my hair, seaweed-moist.

I wait for light.

A ship's shadow passes over me. Something in the water sticks to my arms, gums my scales. A black ink coils downwards. Surface light disappears. I struggle through oil to the rock where we always meet.

My lover waits for me.

Somewhere. I would not see her if she swam towards me. I haunt the spot where we lay. *I have a way to help you breathe*, she said. *You have shared with me your shells and the blazing hearth inside you. I want to show you my sun and lay you down on my bed.* She does not come. The beach is empty. I lick a rock to chase a taste remnant of her. I taste petrol. Swallow saltwater to wash it. Choke on kerosene.

My heart guides me.

When the water clears. When she walks the path at night to reach home before sunrise. When every plastic bag will stop looking like her palm, translucent underwater beyond the sea shelf.

I am waiting.

Cradled

The Pari, tiny protectors made of air

A presence floats to me from the smoke and takes my right hand. My left hand holds my daughter's. An electric shock on the marble floor. Bright lights when the power is out. My head has ached since January. The presence nestles into me on our small bed like she belongs there. Light on my heavy chest. I stay up all night inhaling the vanishing scents on the pillowcase.

In the morning she rustles through the wall and re-enters the room, reforming like a gentle breeze. She whispers me out of bed, out the door, out the gate, down the road, down another road, another. The school stands in front of me. She says, *look right at the makaiwala and hear your daughter begging for corn*. I buy one packet of corn for myself, one for her, one for my left hand where I tugged my daughter through the traffic.

At the pier ledge we swing our legs over and watch boats on the horizon. Families are laughing all around us. Corn sticks in my throat. Lemon and salt. Sweat. Crisp waves. Air alive. A second skin of smoke lifts up.

Cast Out

Banbh and Manh, twin sisters, half women, half-hellish

In we paw through the scrub for figs and apricots. We make slings from our dupattas to carry them back home. And when I run out of material I weigh down our shalwar with papayas. And when I run out of space there I poke bunches of grapes into my hair. The crows land on my head as I pick and peck away. We shoo. They peck. They swarm. Ants crawl up my arms, sucking at the sweet ferment. In August we all forage for food, no cover from the heat. There are mouths to feed. Papayas for the kashigars, figs for the dhobi's children, mashed apricots for the darzi's new baby. In the morning we will be long gone. They will smell mangoes ripened in the sun. Cheekoo milk, sticky on their fingers.

Out of the scrub we make our way back to the village. I laugh at the thorny mess of her clothes. She laughs at the nest in my hair and shoos a beetle off. The water is finished. The village is dustier and emptier as we walk in laden with fruit. Exchange a curious glance. Then, a pelt. Another. A rock hits our hip bone and a papaya tumbles out. I look up to faces contorted in terror. I look behind—there is no dust storm or desert beast, only brambles. They do not stare behind or around, but directly at us, eyes wide and hands ready to lob more rocks. *Please! Please* — my sister clasps my wrist. We run and run until in the scrub there is no one except crows and each other. I hold my sister and tell her we will find our way. Whatever our way is.

The Bells Creep In
The Churail, a witch-like figure

I.

She is a woman, always a woman. Her name, churail, sends shivers down your spine. You may know her from Karakoram mountains, city grave-yards, crossroads, the chill you feel walking under a tree past maghrib. You may know her as she haunts empty highways and stretches of coast-line at night when the last beach hut turns its lights off. You may know her from your grandmother's tongue as she tells you the story of how she barely escaped. Your grandmother made it back to the city but her friend did not.

When you are pregnant and in labour you are afraid. If you die right then you will become her, churail. You scream as a baby pushes out between your legs and hope you don't die. You hope because this is the only thing you can do. The nurse hands you the child you shared your body with for nine months. All you feel is relief that you are alive. You could die tomor-row and leave the baby behind, but you would not mind. All that matters right now is that you are alive.

Once you were driving on National Highway 10 back to Karachi from a day trip in Hub. The music was loud and the windows were down. Perhaps this was your first mistake. You saw her appear in the time it took you to blink. Your father swerved and sped up and when you turned back, she was gone. You swear you heard the chime of anklets follow you long after you'd crossed the border between Sindh and Balochistan.

Sometimes she's hunched over, shedding skin on the sand, spitting words with a black tongue. Other times she's a bride, arms laden with bangles clinking with every step. Sometimes she wears a white shroud. Other times she roams naked.

When you're in the kitchen rolling roti she enters your straying thoughts. When you're drifting to sleep on the charpai when the light is gone again she enters your nightmares. If you fall asleep and don't wake up you will become her, a witch who haunts her husband, her brother, her father. If someone comes and slits your throat as you sleep you will become her.

II.

Once you were turtle-watching and you saw her. Just a dark silhouette standing where the Arabian sea laps on the shore. She wasn't doing anything but standing. Your mother cautioned you not to go near. Not to ask the lost figure on Hawkesbay Beach if she needed help. You couldn't see her face so you didn't know if she was hunched over or shrouded, or if a tika dangled from her forehead. Her dark hair, sleek, blended into the night. Your only clue, the clinking jewelry. This, too, swallowed by the cacophony of waves.

When you marry and move into your husband's house you are afraid. You obey every word your in-laws say because if you don't, they say you will become her. A woman thirsting for revenge, they say. If you yell back when they shout at you, or if you don't satisfy your husband, he says you will become her. You love your husband and don't want to seek revenge on him. You'd just like to die peacefully. You don't want to drain your youngest brother of blood. You don't want your father to lie in a pool of his own blood with your nail marks still red across his face.

You are a woman and you are awake.

Churail and Car Passing on Road — Jute, dried flowers, reclaimed wedding invitations, rock

The Word Itself

*The Budha Baba, an old man who takes away
disobedient children*

Ami says, *finish every last dana on your plate,* or else the Budha Baba will
take you away.

He, six, licks every drop of salan off
his fingers. Lifts up his plate and licks
it clean. He taps his foot against the
chair's leg. Ami is reorganizing the
freezer. Abu is washing the dishes.
He tiptoes up the stairs, biting his lip
as the top step creaks. A shadow at
the end of the corridor. He runs into
his room where the lights are still on.

The bell rings. She, eight, jumps in
her seat. Sits up straight. Peers out
the window into the dark garden.
The figure walking up the path
is dark. His white beard shines
without the streetlamps. She clicks
her nails together and watches her
empty plate. The click of amber
beads rattling as he walks.

Abu gets up to answer the door.

A Day in the Life

The Jinn, beings of fire

I meet my friend for chai past midnight. The dhaba bursts with humans lounging back, playing ludo, raucous laughter buzzes. We sit squished between two tables. The human to my right shudders as I take my seat. *I swear there's a jinn here or something*, he says, eyes wide. My friend and I roll our eyes.

» *That was three-hundred years ago. You would think the humans realized it wasn't all of us.*

» *These creatures will forget what they did in the morning but will be scared of us till qayamat.*

Meow, meow. A cat curls around my leg. I pet its matted fur.

» *What if I messed around with the human boy a bit?*

» *Please don't.*

» *A bit of flute. It will be gentle.*

» *He will scream at the mysterious sound coming from his side. We are here to enjoy.*

I pout and let the cat go. It pads away, eyes glowing into the night. I finish my last dreg. Malai sticks to the side of my cup. My friend and I walk down the street together, stopping at the cluster of neem trees at the roundabout. I say goodbye to my friend.

Curling into a branch, I play my flute. Humans stroll through the trees. They stop, look at the ground, look around, but they never glance upwards. The cat brushes around their ankles. It looks up at me, teeth bared, and mewls. I huff. The humans shudder.

» *I am just enjoying myself.*

» *You know exactly what you are doing. I stop the music. Daybreak is close. The cat leaps onto my branch and curls against me.*

I stop the music. Daybreak is close. The cat leaps onto my branch and curls against me.

The Wandering Falcon
The Stories of Lal Shahbaz Qalandar

Saints are an important part of Sindh's spiritual and cultural heritage. Although many Sufi saints are celebrated in Sindh, we have chosen to highlight a few who have a strong presence through storytelling and song.

The stories of Lal Shahbaz Qalandar are as sprawling as the saint himself. His name translates to "the Wandering Red Falcon," which should tell you something about his life. He was born Usman Marwandi in modern-day Iran. He wandered from Makkah and Madina to Cairo and Damascus, and spent some time in Karbala before he finally settled in Sehwan. For 800 years, the shrine of Lal Shahbaz Qalandar has remained a site of pilgrimage for thousands of people every day.

Even when he settled, he did not settle. Lal Shahbaz Qalandar came to Sehwan, which was already bursting with fakirs, and asked to enter the city. The fakirs turned him away with a metaphor. A bowl filled with milk that, if jostled, would spill over. The message was clear: there was not enough room for even one more fakir in Sehwan. Lal Shahbaz Qalandar responded with another metaphor. He placed a flower on the bowl of milk and watched it float around. Like the flower, he would float around Sehwan, not disturbing what was already in the city.

Like its namesake, the song "Lal Meri Pat" has travelled throughout Pakistan and crossed into India. "Lal Meri Pat" is around 100 years old and praises his legacy. Sung by musicians while people belt out the chorus, the song captures the spiritual energy the saint exuded in his life.

In one story, Lal Shahbaz Qalandar was sitting praying in the desert. Two sticks were set in the sand in front of him. A wandering man happened to stumble upon the saint praying. Deep in his reverie of one day becoming a king, the man walked over the sticks. He jerked back to reality and found himself out of the desert and in a bustling city, in front of an ornate door. A crowd had gathered there and told him that the king had died. The city needed a new ruler. At that exact moment, a huma bird

flew down and perched itself on the man's head. It was believed that the huma bird could predict the next king. The man ruled the city for seven years, until he wandered back to the door through which he had entered the city. He pushed the door open and stepped through. His foot touched sand. He was back in the desert, Lal Shahbaz Qalandar praying on the sand.

The stories of Lal Shahbaz Qalandar go on and on. His presence lingers in flute melodies, in rising bonfire smoke, the hard-stamping feet at Sehwan.

Living Folklore
Date: 12th century
Place: Sehwan, Sindh
Shrine: Sehwan, Sindh

Float

in Sehvastan
he becomes a flower
on a milk bowl
                    floating

amongst the city's inhabitants. Floats

                                        to market
                to temple of Shiva

                        to forts
                        and forts
and forts
                    because forts
hold secrets
and stories.

teaches the movements of Karbala

            and everyone dances, one foot
            bounces up, then the other. Toes drag
            on sun-hardened clay

Sehvastan becomes Sehwan
becomes the place where he dies and now

            there is a shrine because

what is a saint
when forgotten

what is a saint
without a shrine

Petals and Milk – Dried orchids, milk, matka

The Palla Fish

The Stories of Jhulelal

Wandering through the lands of the Indus River is Jhulelal, a deity with many names and visages. A difficult figure to untangle, Jhulelal might be called Zinda Pir, Varundev, or Darya Pir depending on where you go. Our first familiarity with him was through the song "Lal Meri Pat," which had deep and widespread cultural significance. In this song, Jhulelal appears incarnated as Sufi saint Lal Shahbaz Qalandar. The lyrics go:

> *Rakhio Bala Jhoole Laalan*
> *O Laal Meri . . .*
> *O Laal Meri Pat*
> *Rakhio Bala Jhoole Laalan*

By playing with the word lal (which means "red" in Urdu), the song blurs the distinction between Jhulelal and Lal Shahbaz Qalandar, and thus between Islam and Hinduism. Instead, the song centres on divine union, a theme spread across Sindhi folklore touching on the union of spirit, love, and death.

Jhulelal came to Sindh at a time when Hindus faced the threat of extinction in Sindh. He was born in the tenth century near Thatta on the banks of the Indus River. The Muslim ruler at the time was coercing Hindus to convert to Islam. The Hindu communities got together and prayed to Varundev, the Indus River deity, for help. Varundev's answer was a baby. The skeptical community saw this baby turn into an old bearded man, who saved them from the oppressive ruler. He told the cruel sultan to realize that Hindus respected their religion as he respected his own.

Jhulelal is known as an incarnation of Varundev. As the river deity, his avatar was a palla fish. Sometimes he took the form of a fish, other times he appeared riding on the fish. Images of him in temples, on trucks, and on shop signs all feature the fish. During his lifetime, he gathered both Hindu and Muslim followers. Just as with the Muslim saints, his shrine in

Uderolal in Sindh brings both Hindu and Muslim devotees, who dance together during Cheti Chand, Jhulelal's birthday. Jhulelal's identity is pluralistic, and represents the long-standing coexistence of religions, cultures, and traditions across Sindh.

Living Folklore
Date: 10th century
Place: River Indus Delta, Sindh
Shrine: Uderolal

As Good As an Altar

a story where history defies

        rulebooks happened every century
on repeat. a new incarnation of a god said

    this time is the last

a name is nothing but a farce, a new shrine
to collect. with each one They divide up

     their time granting miracles; so many

missed prayers in Udero Lal while They
were in Nankana Sahib. a river is just

a river is as good an alter

     as something lined with gold. an outline
of a fish made with bone as good

       as carvings now crumbled.

    a story not told to children who find
war instead of asking Them

      give this story a different ending

even if the answer is just

        make your own

Shrine of Jhulelal — Wedding invitation, cloth, tasbih beads, sumac berries,
cardboard

Between a Wish and a Prayer

tie a string to a tree and hope
something will come of it

        not a string but a strip ripped from sari

ami's warm hands
comb through hair, massage in

mustard oil. mouth along to a lullaby she sings

        lal palang par so ja
        ami abu ain gai

        words a braided cord looped
        on low-hanging branch

I hum to sleep my own child
and she dreams of threads

        ends of dupattas and saris
        all blow in the wind

collide with other prayers,
another voice sings

        the story of a grave in the middle of a lake
        the story of a necklace tossed in a desert
        the story of melted clay in a river

the tree sags with the weight of wishes,
of travellers who trek through mountains
and sand, through lost
archaeological ruins and crumbling

Mannat Tree – Stones, wire, embroidery floss, handmade beads with old magazines   99

tombs, a search that yields
nothing but copper coins

before they come
home again

About *Reth aur Reghistan*

Women Wide Awake is part of *Reth aur Reghistan*, a multidisciplinary arts project started by two Pakistani sisters. The project explores folklore from Sindh in a contemporary context through sculpture and poetry.

Reth aur Reghistan translates to "Sand and Desert," capturing the unique landscape of these stories and our childhood. In this project we decided to bring together our collective interest in crafting and storytelling to share folktales in a way that is meaningful to the present using pieces from the past. Growing up in Karachi, we played together in a full house with our parents, dadi, dada, and phupi. Our dadi carefully saved items like pieces of sari cloth, broken jewelry, and colourful wedding invitations. We played, crafted, and used these items to create characters and stories.

As adults, we had acquired an abundance of materials that had their own stories and histories, which made them even more exciting to work with. Our artistic process values memory as a creative medium. We consider the personal memories embedded within each material as we interpret folktales. For example, we created the figure of Mai Kolachi with shells collected from a beach during childhood trips, close to where her story originated. We dressed the bold sisters Moomal and Soomal in pieces of our dadi's red sari that she gave us once it was torn.

Our experiences growing up in Karachi, and our intimate connection with the stories that the city holds led us to choose Karachi and the province of Sindh as our place of research. We travelled to Karachi for this project in 2019 and produced the manuscript in 2020. During the editing process in late summer 2022, Pakistan was hit with some of the worst flooding it has seen in its history. Sindh was one of the provinces most affected, leading to the destruction of communities and mass displacement. The monsoon season occurs every year and the impacts of today's climate crisis will continue to affect this region. Relief efforts to provide food, shelter, rehabilitation, medicine, and more are ongoing. For all *Reth*

aur Reghistan workshops and events, we will be continuing to collect and donate funds to support rehabilitation efforts.

To learn more about *Reth aur Reghistan*, see our website, sculpturalstorytelling.com.

Glossary

ajrak: a form of block printing traditional to Sindh

chadar: a cloth used as a head covering or cover

chand raat: the night of a full moon

cheekoo: sweet fruit from Karachi

Cheti Chand: a festival marking the beginning of the lunar new year for Sindhi Hindus

dhaba: a roadside restaurant, very commonly found in South Asia

dhobi: washerperson

dupatta: traditional fabric loosely draped around the chest or head

fakir: a title for those who devote their life to spiritual purposes

kameez: traditional clothing worn by women

Karbala: a city in Iraq that is a central site of Shia Muslims

kashikari: the art of hand-painting ceramics

kurta: traditional clothing worn by men

lakh: a unit of measurement of a hundred thousand

magarmach: crocodile

makaiwala: vender who sells corn

malai: cream

mannat: an intention or wish placed through an act of devotion or prayer

ralli: traditional patchwork quilt made by women in areas of Sindh

takht: traditional bed-like seating

wazir: a high-ranking officer

Research

We conducted formal and informal interviews with individuals from different academic, cultural, and creative fields, gathered stories, and asked people why folklore was important to their work. We would like to thank the following individuals for generously sharing their knowledge of history and folklore with us: Dr Kaleemullah Lashari, Dr Asma Ibrahim, Arieb Azhar, Fakir Mohammad Ismail Mirjut, Attiya Dawood, Dr Masooma M Shakir, and Suhaee Abro.

Early on in our research we came across the well-known Sufi poet and saint Shah Abdul Latif Bhittai. He significantly influenced the folklore of Sindh through his *Shah Jo Risalo*, a compilation of poetry that includes 30 surs (verses) that are sung accompanied by music. In his *Risalo* are the stories of the Seven Queens who appear in *Women Wide Awake*. Whether these centuries-old folktales are alive because of Bhittai's poetry is uncertain, but he gave a vehicle through his work to experience through song and imaginative language, the longing, strength, and love of these women.

We visited the following sites, museums and archives:
- » Karachi: the Sindh Archives and Mohatta Palace
- » Islamabad: the Lok Virsa Museum
- » Bhit Shah: the Shrine of Shah Abdul Latif Bhittai and the Bhit Shah Museum
- » Umerkot: the Umerkot Fort, a Jogi community on the outskirts of the city, and the Umerkot Museum
- » Bhambhore, the archaeological site of the village of Sasui and the Bhambhore Museum
- » Thatta: the Makli Necropolis and the Shah Jahan Masjid

We referred to the following books:
- » *Rhythms of the Lower Indus: Perspectives on the Music of Sindh,*

edited by Zohra Yusuf, Department of Culture and Tourism, Government of Sindh, 1988.

» *Shah Abdul Latif of Bhit*, by H T Sorley, Oxford University Press, 1967.

» Also, stories shared through Sindhi Sangat, a non-profit organization dedicated to sharing and promoting Sindhi culture

More resources on folklore in Sindh and other regions in Pakistan can be found on our website, sculpturalstorytelling.com/resources.

Acknowledgements

Thank you to the Canada Council for the Arts, Recommender Grants from the Ontario Arts Council, the City of Ottawa, and the Mississauga Arts Council for funding this project.

Excerpts from this book have appeared in *Room* and *long con magazine*, and have also been featured in *Emergents I: ReRoots* and *Tell Me Who We Were* (3 of Cups Press). A selection of sculptures and poems of figures from Pakistani folklore appeared in our chapbook *Encounter* with Rahila's Ghost Press. Thank you to the journalists and artists who amplified *Reth aur Reghistan* through their practices, including Zool Suleman from *Rungh Cultural Society*, Adeeb Abdul Razak from *Juice*, Sakina Shakil Groppmaier, Aeman Ansari, and Sadiya Ansari.

Thank you to everyone at Mawenzi House for taking a chance on a hybrid manuscript, including Nurjehan Aziz for all the support, M G Vassanji for editing, and Sabrina Pignataro for the design and layout.

Thank you to our friends in Karachi who accompanied us on folklore adventures. To Sheniz Jamohamed and Sanita Fejzić for helping us navigate the grant-writing world. To Sharada Eswar, Florenica Berinstein, and Ruth Howard from Jumblies Theatre & Arts for inspiring our arts practice and inviting us to participate in the Jumblies Artist Residency.

To Abu for letting us turn the living room into our studio space for months. To our little sister Mashal for putting up with endless conversations about folklore. Thank you to our phupi, Sajida Bandukwala, for sowing the seeds of this project. To Mama for crafting with us for this project and in our childhood.

Manahil Bandukwala (she/her), left, is a poet and visual artist. She is the author of *MONUMENT*, and many chapbooks. She enjoys working collaboratively, and in addition to *Reth aur Reghistan*, frequently collaborates with other writers, musicians, and artists in Canada. She holds an MA in English from the University of Waterloo and in 2023, was selected as a Writer's Trust Rising Star by Shani Mootoo. manahilbandukwala.com.

Nimra Bandukwala (she/her), right, is a visual artist and maker of crafts using foraged and found materials. More recently, she has been integrating earth pigments and natural dyes into her practice while exploring the stories and histories behind these materials. She is a recipient of arts grants from the Ontario Arts Council and the Canada Council for the Arts. Nimra has facilitated community-engaged workshops with folks of all ages and abilities in schools and community-based settings. nimrabandukwala.com.